Cinderella

Illustrations by J. L. MACIAS S.

Retold by JANE CARRUTH

Once upon a time there was a merchant who married again when his wife died. His new wife was a proud, cruel woman who hated the merchant's young daughter.

"Cinderella," she said, "will be her new name. Her place is in the kitchen, for she must do the work of a servant." The step-mother had two daughters. They were as proud and cruel as their mother, and very plain. At night they made poor Cinderella curl their hair and then sent her down to the kitchen to sleep on the stone floor, with only her faithful dog to keep her company as she slept.

Now, Cinderella, in her rags, was much prettier than the two Ugly Sisters. This made them very angry and, as the months passed, nothing she could do would please them. One day an invitation came from the palace to attend the Grand Ball the King was giving for his son, the Prince. Cinderella began to dream of going to the ball and this made the Sisters laugh at her.

"The Prince would never look at you in your rags!" they sneered. When at last the day came for the two Ugly Sisters to set out for the ball, Cinderella was at the washtub. "Oh, I do so long to be going to the Ball," she thought as she watched them go. And she sighed and began to cry because she was so sad at being left behind.

Still feeling sad, Cinderella set about the washing-up and it was then that something wonderful happened. Suddenly, there appeared before her the most beautiful lady she had ever seen. "I am your Fairy Godmother," said the beautiful lady.

"Do what I say and you will go to the Ball." Then she told
Cinderella to take a big pumpkin outside and fetch her the
mousetrap, which held six little mice. With a wave of her wand the
Fairy changed the pumpkin into a magnificent golden coach.

The six little mice became six handsome horses and some garden lizards found themselves changed into footmen. Cinderella gasped when she saw that she was no longer in rags but in a gorgeous dress of silk and satin embroidered with sparkling jewels and that on her feet were two dainty glass slippers, the prettiest in the world. "Was she dreaming?" she wondered.

"Remember," said the Fairy. "You must leave the Ball before the hour of midnight strikes or you will lose everything!"

As soon as Cinderella reached the palace, she was escorted into the ballroom. Almost at once, the king's son, the handsome young Prince, invited her to dance with him. All the ladies, who had hoped to dance with the Prince, were jealous.

"Who is she?" they whispered. "How lovely she looks! She must be a grand Princess. No wonder the Prince has eyes only for her!"

Cinderella was so happy dancing with the Prince that she forgot
the Fairy's warning. The palace clock was striking the hour of
twelve when she remembered. And with a cry of dismay she fled
from the ballroom and down the palace steps.

In her haste, she left behind one of her pretty glass slippers. The Prince tried to follow her, but he saw only a poor young girl in rags running down the street followed by six little mice.

Day after day, the Prince thought only of his mysterious Princess. At last he sent out a Proclamation that he would marry the girl who could wear the dainty glass slipper. His Messengers would take the slipper to every house in his kingdom.

When the Royal Messenger arrived at Cinderella's house, the two Ugly Sisters pushed and squeezed their feet into the slipper, but all in vain. But when Cinderella tried on the slipper it proved a perfect fit, and she was taken at once to the palace.

Cinderella and the Prince were married the very next day. Their
wedding was the most magnificent the world had ever seen, and
the happiest girl in the world was, of course, Cinderella.

Published in United States and simultaneously in Canada by Joshua Morris, Inc
431 Post Road East, Westport, CT 0688
Printed in Belgiur

Tom Thumb

Illustrations by J. L. MACIAS S.

Retold by JANE CARRUTH

There was once a woodcutter who had seven sons, the youngest being so tiny that he named him Tom Thumb. When the woodcutter could no longer feed his sons, he took them deep into the forest and left them.

The boys tried to find their way home, but when night fell they knew they were lost. Only little Tom Thumb kept up his spirits and it was he who discovered a huge castle which stood among the trees. "Come on, boys," he cried. "Don't be afraid!"

The woman who came to the castle door had a kind face, but when Tom Thumb asked her to give them food and shelter for the night, she looked afraid. "My husband is a terrible ogre," she said. "It would not be safe for you to stay here."
But Tom Thumb pleaded so hard that at last she let them come in.

They had no sooner sat down to supper when the ogre came home, and the woman had only time to hide the boys under the table before he strode into the kitchen.

"I smell fresh meat!" roared the ogre, and began searching the room. It wasn't long before he found the frightened boys and would have devoured them on the spot if his wife had not given him a big roast sheep to eat instead. "I'll eat them in the morning," he said. And his wife quickly put the boys to bed.

Their beds were in a room next to the ogre's seven daughters, who slept with gold crowns on their heads. That night, Tom Thumb crept into their room and put their crowns on the heads of his sleeping brothers. And it was just as well he did!

In the middle of the night, the wicked ogre stumbled upstairs. Tom Thumb was still wide awake and he heard the ogre mutter, "I must feel for the crowns of gold! I must not cut off the heads of my dear young daughters."

But that is just what the ogre did! It was too dark for him to see and when he touched the crowns he moved away from the boys' room into the room where his daughters were sleeping.

"Quick! We must escape now before the ogre finds what he has done!" Tom told his six brothers, and he led them down the wide stone stairs and out of the castle.

Once outside, they began to run, and they were a long way from the castle by morning. Now, when the ogre discovered what he had done, he fell into a black rage and pulling on his magic seven-league boots he set off in pursuit.

"Hide, hide!" whispered Tom, when suddenly they heard the crashing of branches. "The ogre is not far away." Tom Thumb showed his six frightened brothers where to hide just as the ogre thundered past, and they sighed with relief as he disappeared into the thick forest.

"Now we can follow him," said Tom Thumb bravely. "We shall be safer behind him than in front."

In his wonderful seven-league boots the ogre covered many miles. But at last he grew weary and, stretching himself out across a bridge, he shut his eyes and was soon fast asleep. "There he is," Tom Thumb whispered, when at last the boys caught up with him. "And he has kicked off one of his boots!"

Quickly, Tom told his brothers what he was going to do. "If we take his magic boots," he said, "the ogre will never catch us. Come on, boys, help me!" Tom began to tug at the other boot and his brothers joined in. How heavy it seemed. And how they pulled and tugged until it came off the giant's foot.

The seven-league boots, being magic, fitted anybody who put them on. And soon Tom Thumb was striding along in the ogre's boots, his brothers running and skipping behind. In no time at all their cottage was in sight and there was their mother!

How happy she was to see them again for she was sure that they had been devoured by some wild forest animal. "We must tell your father!" she cried at last. And when the woodcutter came he wept tears of joy to have his children safely home.

The king soon heard about Tom Thumb's adventures and
he was so pleased at his bravery that he appointed him
Royal Messenger. Tom Thumb, in his magic seven-league
boots, was the swiftest of Messengers, and it wasn't long
before his fortune was made!

Published in United States and simultaneously in Canada by Joshua Morris, In
431 Post Road East, Westport, CT 068
Printed in Belgiu

Little Red Riding Hood

Illustrations by J. L. MACIAS S.

Retold by JANE CARRUTH

Once upon a time there was a pretty little girl who lived with her Mummy and Daddy close to a big wood. Everybody called her Red Riding Hood because she always wore a red cape and hood.

On the far side of the big wood lived Red Riding Hood's grandmother and, one day, the little girl set out to visit her.

Little Red Riding Hood loved her grandmother and she was glad her Mummy had filled her basket with honey and cakes to take to her. Her Mummy had told her to go all the way around the wood because of the big bad wolf who lived there. But it was such a sunny day that Red Riding Hood forgot all about the wolf.

She went into the wood and, oh dear, quite soon she met that big bad wolf. "Good morning to you," said the wolf, in a soft, kind voice. "Where are you going?"
"To see my grandmother," said Red Riding Hood. "I'm taking her some honey and cakes because she isn't very well today."

The big bad wolf was very cunning. He pretended to be sad that Red Riding Hood's grandmother was not very well. And he soon found out just where she lived. "You gather some flowers to take to her," he said at last. "I must be off!"

Goodness, how fast that big bad wolf ran through the woods! He did not draw breath until he had found the grandmother's cottage and was knocking at the door. "It's your own Red Riding Hood," he called gently. "Unbolt the door and let me in."

No sooner was the wolf inside than he gobbled up the old lady. Then he wrapped her shawl around his shoulders, put on her pink nightcap and balanced her spectacles on his nose. "Now I'll wait for Red Riding Hood," he thought, as he jumped into bed.

He did not have long to wait. He had only time to pull the cover right up to his face before Red Riding Hood arrived.

"How are you?" she asked, going up to the bed. "I've brought you some pretty flowers and a basket full of good things."

Then Red Riding Hood looked at her grandmother more closely, as the wolf croaked, "Come and give your Granny a kiss, child!"

"But Grandmama, what big ears you have got!"

"All the better to hear you with," said the wolf.

"And, oh Grandmama, what big eyes you have got."

"All the better to see you with," said the wolf.

"And Grandmama, what big teeth you have got!"

"All the better to eat you with," snarled the big bad wolf, and he sprang out of bed.

Poor little Red Riding Hood was so frightened that she dropped her basket and tried to escape. But the wolf caught her and gobbled her up.

Then he felt so heavy with the old lady and Red Riding Hood inside him that he climbed back into bed and fell asleep.

Now, two farm workers had seen the big bad wolf enter the old lady's cottage. "We had better go and find out if she is safe," they said to each other. Imagine their horror when they saw the wolf in bed and the room turned upside down. "The wolf has gobbled up the old lady for sure," said one.

"And the little girl," said the other. "We had better cut him open as fast as we can."

So the two brave men went into the cottage and they cut open the wolf, who was sleeping so heavily that he did not wake up, which was just as well, for out of his big stomach hopped the old lady and after her came little Red Riding Hood!

And while Red Riding Hood and her grandmother ran outside to hide in the woods, the two farm workers filled the wolf's stomach with heavy stones and then sewed it up.

When the big bad wolf did wake up he felt so heavy and thirsty that he staggered out of the cottage and made his way to the pond for a drink. But the stones moved inside his stomach. He over-balanced and fell into the water and soon drowned.

When the old lady heard the wolf was dead, she took Red Riding
Hood back to the cottage. She hugged and kissed the little girl and
said that all the excitement had made her feel much better. Then
they tidied up the room and had cakes and honey for tea. So, after
all, it was a happy day for them both.

Published in United States and simultaneously in Canada by Joshua Morris, Inc.
431 Post Road East, Westport, CT 06880
Printed in Belgium

The Sleeping Beauty

Illustrations by J. L. MACIAS S.

Retold by JANE CARRUTH

Once upon a time there lived a King and Queen who longed, with all their hearts, for a child of their own.

After many years, and to their great joy, the Queen gave birth to a beautiful baby girl. All the people rejoiced with them.

"We must invite all our friends to the Christening Party," said the Queen. "And we must invite all the fairies."
Alas, the King forgot to send an invitation to one of the oldest and most important fairies in the land and so he had no special present made for her.

The fairies who came to the Christening bestowed upon the baby many wonderful gifts. Beauty and grace and intelligence would all be hers as she grew up. Then, suddenly, the oldest fairy in the land appeared, dressed in black and with a face twisted in rage. "I, too, have a gift for the royal baby!" she screamed. "She will die from the prick of a spindle when she is fifteen years old!" And she laughed loudly.

Now the youngest of the fairies had not yet bestowed her gift on the little Princess.

"Be of good heart," she told the horrified King and Queen. "The child will not die. She will fall into a deep sleep which will last one hundred years, and then a king's son shall wake her." But the royal parents could not be comforted and the King said that every spindle in the land must be burned. Any person caught using a spinning wheel would be put to death.

Years passed and the Princess grew into a beautiful young girl, greatly loved by all who knew her. On her fifteenth birthday her parents took her to their castle in the country, where she was free to walk and play in the gardens, and ride her pony along country lanes.

One day, the Princess set out to explore all the small rooms at the very top of the castle. In one, she came upon an old woman, busy spinning. "Let me try, good mother!" she cried.

Now the old woman had not heard of the wicked fairy's curse or even that the King had a daughter. "Take it then, my pretty child," she said, handing her spindle to the Princess. Almost at once the girl felt a sharp prick and, with a small cry, she fell to the ground and lay as if dead. Terrified, the old woman rushed from her turret room, shouting for help.

Sadly, the King and Queen told their servants to carry the Princess to her bed-chamber. Then a strange thing happened.

All who were in the castle that day fell into a deep sleep. Even the cats and dogs and the little doves went to sleep.

This was the work of the youngest fairy, who came to the castle in her chariot drawn by dragons. So powerful was her magic that even the cook fell asleep in the very act of tasting the soup, and the jesters in the middle of telling jokes! One hundred years passed and all around the castle had grown a thick hedge of briars and thorns.

One day, a king's son was hunting in the forest and when he heard the story from an old woodcutter of the Sleeping Beauty in the strange, silent castle, he made up his mind to cut through the thick hedge and break into the castle so that he might find out for himself if the story was true.

The Prince drew his sword, but it was not needed, for a path appeared and he had only to follow it to reach the castle gates.

All was still and silent as the young Prince began his search for the Sleeping Beauty. He came upon her at last, lying on a bed of silver, her golden hair spread about her shoulders. And so lovely was she that the Prince lost his heart to her.

"So the story of the Sleeping Beauty is true," he said to himself, as he stood gazing at her. "How wonderfully beautiful she is!" Slowly, he approached the bed. Then he bent down and gently kissed the Princess. At the touch of his lips, she opened her eyes, and the sleeping castle came to bustling life.

The Princess, on waking, knew that she too had found her true love and the very next day they were married. So beautiful did she look on her Wedding Day that the Prince did not even notice that her wedding gown was one hundred years out of fashion!

Published in United States and simultaneously in Canada by Joshua Morris, Inc.
431 Post Road East, Westport, CT 06880
Printed in Belgium

Puss-in-Boots

Illustrations by J. L. MACIAS S.

Retold by JANE CARRUTH

There was once a poor miller who, when he died, left all he had to his three sons. The eldest had the mill, the second son had the donkey and Jack, the youngest, was left the cat.

"How can I earn my living with only a cat to help me?" Jack said sadly. "It is more likely we shall starve together, Puss."

"Do not be down-hearted, Master," said Puss. "Just get me a pair of tall boots and a sack and put your trust in me."

"Oh very well," said Jack. "But I don't see how you can help me."

As soon as he had the boots and the sack, Puss set out for the woods, where he knew there were some very fine rabbits. After laying a trap for the rabbits by putting a fresh carrot inside his sack, he hid behind a tree, and it wasn't long before a rabbit came along.

No sooner was the plump little rabbit inside the sack than Puss pulled the string he was holding and the rabbit was caught. Now it was well known that the King simply adored rabbit pie and Puss headed straight for the palace. When he stood before the King, he said, "Your Majesty, my master, the Marquis of Carabas, has sent you a gift of a fine rabbit." The King was delighted with such a thoughtful gift and begged Puss-in-Boots to thank his noble master.

Puss-in-Boots went on catching rabbits and taking them to the King until he became quite a favourite at court. He soon learned that the King and the lovely Princess went for a drive in their coach at the same time each day. "You must bathe in the river close to the bridge," Puss told his master one morning. "I will hide your old clothes."

Greatly puzzled, Jack obeyed and was astonished to see Puss on the bridge and stopping the royal coach. "My master, the Marquis of Carabas, has had all his fine clothes stolen," he told the King.

"He will have the best suit in my wardrobe," cried the King, and he sent a messenger back to the palace to fetch it. In his new clothes the miller's son looked very handsome and he was invited to ride in the coach with the lovely Princess. Meanwhile, Puss ran on ahead.

As soon as Puss came to a band of workers in the fields, he said, "You must tell the King that you work for the noble Marquis of Carabas. If you don't, I'll eat you up!"

Now Puss was making for a great castle where he knew a certain ogre
lived. The ogre was very rich and very conceited. He was just about to sit
down to his dinner when Puss-in-Boots arrived. "I hear," said Puss, "that
you have wonderful powers. You can change yourself into a huge lion if
you wish."

"That is very true," smiled the ogre. And did so immediately. Puss got such a fright that he scrambled up the nearest curtain and hung on for dear life, while the lion roared and snarled at him.

"Now I know you have truly wonderful powers," he was just able to squeak.

Then he went on, "It's easy for a great big fellow to turn himself into a great big lion. I wonder if you could change yourself into a tiny mouse? That must be too difficult even for you!"

"Nothing easier," said the ogre, and did so at once.

Puss made a dive for the mouse and gobbled him up!

Now the castle was his, and Puss climbed the ramparts and waved his fine hat to stop the royal coach as it came clattering past. "Welcome, welcome!" he shouted. "Welcome to the castle of the noble Marquis of Carabas!"

No wonder the King began to think the Marquis must be a very rich man indeed!

In the great banqueting hall all was ready for a magnificent feast, and the miller's son, who had quite fallen in love with the Princess, led her to the table. The King and Puss-in-Boots watched the pair and both decided, almost at the same time, that it would be an excellent idea if they got married. After the feasting the young couple walked in the garden and Jack, the poor miller's son, proposed there and then to the Princess.

There was no happier young man in the whole world than Jack when the Princess declared her love for him. Puss-in-Boots was happy too. And, after the wedding, he was given a special velvet cushion of his own, and salmon and cream every day.

Published in United States and simultaneously in Canada by Joshua Morris, Inc.
431 Post Road East, Westport, CT 06880
Printed in Belgium

Snow-White
and the 7 Dwarfs

Illustrations by J. L. MACIAS S.

Retold by JANE CARRUTH

Once upon a time there was a young Princess called Snow-White whose mother had died soon after she was born.

Snow-White's father, the King, married again. His new Queen was a strange woman, tall and beautiful, but with the powers of a witch. In a secret room at the top of the palace were hidden her Book of Magic Spells, her raven and her black pot of magic potions.

On the wall hung a magic mirror. Every day the Queen looked into her magic mirror and asked it the same question: "Mirror, mirror on the wall, who is the fairest of us all?" And the mirror would reply: "You, O Queen, are the fairest of all."

Then one day, the magic mirror
told the proud Queen that
Snow-White was now the fairest
in the land. "Then she must die!" cried the Queen in a rage. And she sent for
one of her huntsmen and told him to take the girl into the forest and kill her.
But the huntsman could not do such a cruel thing.

He told Snow-White to hide away in the forest. Soon after he left her, Snow-White came upon a little cottage among the trees. When she opened the door and looked inside, she saw seven little chairs around the untidy breakfast table.

In the room upstairs, Snow-White found seven little beds and, with a huge yawn, she lay down and was soon fast asleep. She was still asleep when the seven little dwarfs came home from the gold and diamond mines where they worked. How surprised they were to find Snow-White in their cottage.

"Who can she be?" they asked each other in wonderment.

The dwarfs waited patiently until Snow-White opened her eyes. When they heard her sad story, the eldest said, "You may stay here if you promise to cook for us and keep the cottage tidy."

"I should love to," said Snow-White. And from that day she became the dwarfs' housekeeper and took care of them.

Now the wicked Queen soon learned from her magic mirror that Snow-White still lived and, disguising herself as an old country woman, she hurried to the cottage. "I have brought you a lovely rosy-red apple, pretty one," she croaked when she saw Snow-White.
Alas, the apple contained a deadly poison.

No sooner did Snow-White take a bite of the poisoned apple than she fell to the ground. The seven dwarfs wept bitter tears when they came home from the mines and found her.

"This is the work of the evil Queen," said one, shaking his head. "She is too beautiful to lie buried in the cold earth," said another. "Let us make her a glass coffin so that all who pass this way may see how beautiful she is!"

And that is what the seven sad little dwarfs did! Day and night, two sat by the glass coffin on guard until, one day, a handsome Prince came riding through the forest.

The Prince fell so deeply in love with Snow-White that he begged the dwarfs to allow his servants to take her back to his palace. And, at last, they agreed. But when the glass coffin was moved the piece of poisoned apple, lodged in her throat, fell from her mouth. She was alive! Overcome with joy, the Prince told Snow-White that he loved her with all his heart.

Soon after, the noble Prince carried Snow-White away on his white charger. The seven little dwarfs were sad to see her go, but when they attended her wedding the next week, they danced for joy!

Published in United States and simultaneously in Canada by Joshua Morris, Inc.
431 Post Road East, Westport, CT 06880
Printed in Belgium